FOLLOW THE LEADER

PICTURES AND WORDS BY
MIELA FORD

GREENWILLOW BOOKS, NEW YORK

The full-color photographs were
reproduced from 35-mm slides.
The text type is ITC Kabel Medium.

Printed in Singapore by Tien Wah Press
First Edition 10 9 8 7 6 5 4 3 2 1

LIBRARY OF CONGRESS CATALOGING-IN-PUBLICATION DATA

Ford, Miela.
Follow the leader / words and pictures by
Miela Ford.
p.   cm.
Summary: Two polar bears in the zoo
play follow-the-leader.
ISBN 0-688-14654-6 (trade)
ISBN 0-688-14655-4 (lib. bdg.)
[1. Polar bear—Fiction.   2. Bears—Fiction.]
I. Title.   PZ7.F75322Fo   1996
[E]—dc20   95-40886   CIP   AC

FOR
DORIS AND BOB

Let's go play.

Follow me!

I'm the leader today.

First do this.

Now over the rock.

All the way.

Wow!

Down the hill fast!

Come on.

You can do it.

That's right.

Up and over.

Now down the hill.

Don't be scared.

On your mark, get set—

Go!

Hooray! You did it.

Now up again

and back inside.

You can lead tomorrow.

MIELA FORD grew up in Philadelphia, where she was born. She graduated from the Philadelphia College of Art. Her first book for children was <u>Little Elephant</u>, illustrated with photographs by her mother, Tana Hoban. This was followed by the popular <u>Sunflower</u>, illustrated by Sally Noll, and <u>Bear Play</u>, the first book illustrated with Miela Ford's own photographs.